Trigger Goes Hunting

Written by Dean S. Bennion

Illustrated by Adrian VanderHoeven

Copyright © 2018 Dean S. Bennion
Published by Papa Slade's Creations

Designed by Vince Pannullo
Illustrated by Adrian VanderHoeven

Printed in the United States of America by RJ Communications.

ISBN: 978-1-73284-280-9

 **www.triggergoesoutdoors.com**

This book is dedicated to all
my grandchildren.
May you be fortunate enough to
hunt with a friend like Trigger.

Trigger is a dog who lives on a farm.
He's furry and cuddly and chock-full of charm.

He loves running and jumping and chasing jackrabbits.
If you toss him a ball, he's sure to go grab it.

With his nose, he can find things hidden under a pile,
(Trigger can smell pheasants hiding for over a mile).

There are lots of things that
Trigger loves to do,

But his favorite thing of all is
hunting with his best friend Sue.

Each fall when the leaves turn, it's always the same,
Sue loads up her truck in search of wild game.

Trigger waits patiently wagging his tail,
Until the truck is all loaded and then without fail,
Sue whistles her signal that it's time to get in,
And Trigger comes running with his big puppy grin.

When they get to the field, he starts sniffing the ground,
Carefully smelling if there are game birds around.
If he catches a whiff of pheasant or quail,
Trigger let's his friend know with a special wag of his tail.

Then off they go searching till they find just the right spot,
And the birds flush from cover, and Sue lines up her shot.
With a boom and a bang she gets two from the brood,
And that puts young Trigger in a retrieving mood.

He runs right to the place where the birds hit the ground,
And he doesn't stop looking until they're both found.

He carries them back to Sue with a smile
And they do it all over - mile after mile.
Trigger loves to go hunting, this much is true,
But hunting is good for other reasons too.

Hunting is good because it helps you stay fit.
It's good exercise to hike and not just to sit.

Hunting gets you out into nature and teaches you things,
Like which plants can be eaten and which ones can sting.

If you become a good hunter and learn to be stealthy,
You might be rewarded with tasty food that is healthy.

Trigger may not understand why hunting is done.
He does it because he knows hunting is fun

But Sue understands what all good hunters do,
That we all should work hard, so that someday....
You can go hunting, with your best friend too.

Trigger's getting ready for his next big adventure.

Find out what's next at
www.triggergoesoutdoors.com

Trigger's Tips on Taking Kids Hunting

1) Be Prepared

2) Be Safe

3) Be Positive

4) Be a Teacher

5) Remember Why You Are There

    a. Adults: it's all about the kids.

    b. Kids: it's all about the snacks.

Hunting Notes

A) "Hunting is an age-old sport that combines physical with nutrition. Hunters can enjoy the sport, commune with nature, and bring home a feast to their families." ("Top 10 Health Benefits of Hunting" http://www.healthfitnessrevolution.com/top-10-health-benefits-hunting/)

B) Properly harvested and prepared wild game is delicious and an excellent source of organic, free range protein. While out in the field, hunters learn about, and often gather other edible plants that support a healthy diet. Mountain Huckleberries and Chanterelle Mushrooms in the Pacific Northwest are personal favorites of the author.

C) Sportsmen and women are very mindful of the environment and donate hundreds of thousands of hours annually to educate others, improve habitat, clean up litter and improve the earth for everyone.

D) In 2011 there were 37.4 million people over the age of 16 who hunted or fished in the United States. They spent approximately 90 billion dollars on hunting and fishing related purchases. Spending by hunters specifically, generates $5.4 billion in state and local taxes. If you add in Federal taxes paid by hunters the number doubles to $11.8 billion They generate roughly $3 billion dollars a year for conservation. (Source America's Sporting Heritage: Fueling the American Economy — The Congressional Sportsmen's Foundation)

E) "By paying the Federal excise tax on hunting equipment, hunters are contributing hundreds of millions of dollars for conservation programs that benefit many wildlife species, both hunted and non-hunted." For example, "Proceeds from the Federal Duck Stamp, a required purchase for migratory waterfowl hunters, have purchased more than five million acres of habitat for the refuge system (2005 statistics only); lands that support waterfowl and many other wildlife species" "Local hunting clubs and national conservation organizations work to protect the future of wildlife by setting aside thousands of acres of habitat and speaking up for conservation in our national and state capitals." (Excerpts from the US Fish & Wildlife website page titled "What do hunters do for conservation?")

F) "A Labrador retriever's sense of smell may be up to a million times greater than ours" ("Your Labrador's Sense of Smell", by Pippa, November 27, 2013 http://www.thelabradorsite.com/your-labradors-sense-of-smell/)

The End